The Girl who got out of Bed

Betsy Childs

Illustrated by Dan Olson

Childpress Books

To my goddaughters.
—B.C.

To Jasmine.
—D.O.

Shirley loved her big girl bed. It was covered in a bright patchwork quilt. Her bunny, Mrs. Bumpers, sat on top of it. But Shirley had a problem…

Shirley would not stay in her bed.

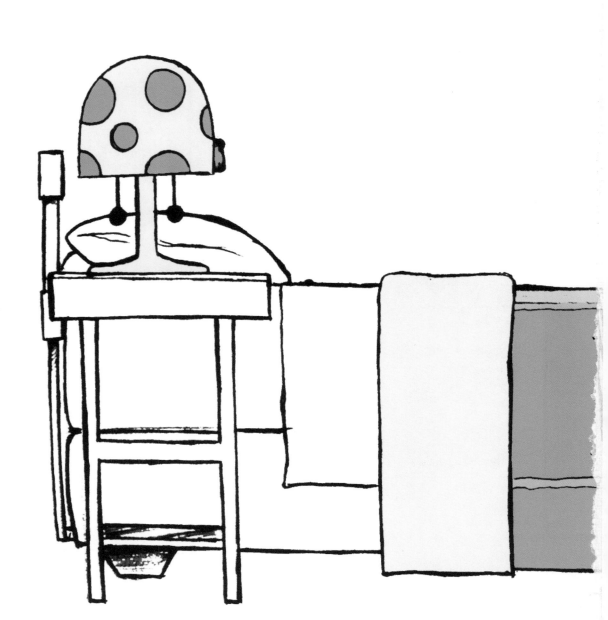

Each night, Mom and Dad listened to Shirley say her prayers and then tucked her in bed with a kiss.

Then they turned on her ladybug light and left the door cracked.

Shirley was alone in her bed with Mrs. Bumpers. Shirley did not like being alone.

Shirley got out of bed.

She padded down the hall. She could hear Mom and Dad watching television. She thought that if she crept in very quietly, they would not know she was there. She held her breath.

But Mom and Dad had excellent hearing. Dad turned off the television. Mom looked at Shirley and raised her eyebrows.

"I forgot something!" Shirley said.

"What did you forget?" asked Dad.

"I forgot how to say my ABCs," said Shirley.

"Yes, that's it! I forgot what comes after G."

"H," said Dad. "H comes after G."

"Oh, yes!" said Shirley. "Thank you!"

"Now," said Dad, "you must get back in bed."

Shirley obeyed her Dad and went back to bed. She looked around the room. She wanted someone to talk to her, but Mrs. Bumpers never talked. The ladybug light glowed silently without a word.

Shirley got out of bed.

This time, no one was in the family room. She found Mom in the kitchen starting the dishwasher. "Mom," she said, "My Band-Aid is getting old." "You can have a new one tomorrow. Remember, one Band-Aid per boo-boo per day." "Oh," said Shirley. "Now go get back in bed," said Mom.

Before Shirley made it back into her bed, she thought of one more thing. She found Dad checking his email.

"Dad, I need to call Nana!" she said. "It is her birthday! Yes, it is her birthday today!"

Dad looked at her. "Today is not Nana's birthday. And Nana and Pop-pop are already asleep. You cannot call them."

So Shirley padded down the hall back to her room.

Shirley lay in her bed for a few minutes and played with the zipper on her jammies. She flipped her pillow over to the cool side. She counted the teeth in her mouth.

She got out of bed.

The hall was dark, but she found Mom and Dad in their bed, reading.

"Shirley," her Dad spoke before she could say anything, "You may not get up again. I will take you back to your bed."

He tucked the little girl under her quilt and said, "Shirley, would you like for it to be morning time?"

"Oh, yes!" said Shirley. "I like morning time."

"I will tell you a secret," said Dad. "I will tell you how to make morning time come."

"Tell me!" said Shirley.

"You must put your head on your pillow and close your eyes. Start to count," Dad said, "If you open your eyes and it is still night time, you did not count high enough. You must close your eyes and start over.

"But if you do this, morning will come right away."

"Oh boy!" said Shirley.

After Dad left, she gave it a try. She and Mrs. Bumpers put their heads on the pillow. Shirley closed her eyes and counted to three.

She opened her eyes, but it was still night time.

So she closed them again and counted to eight. She kept counting. Nine, ten, eleven, twelve…Shirley counted and counted.

Finally, she opened her eyes …

There was light coming through her window! It was morning time!

Shirley ran down the hall. She found Mom and Dad in the kitchen drinking coffee. "It worked!" shouted Shirley. "It is morning time!" Mom and Dad smiled.
"Yes, Shirley," Dad said, "now you know what to do to make the morning come."
"I can't wait to go to bed and do it again!" said Shirley.

"Don't worry," said Mom, giving Shirley a big hug. "Bedtime will roll around before you know it!"

The End

Murray is almost four years old, and he cries over everything. An experience with a slingshot and a sparrow helps him learn that it's okay to cry when you're sad, but it's best not to cry when you're mad. A sweet story and tool to help children learn self-control!

Paperback
ISBN-10: 1467996440
ISBN-13: 978-1467996440

Kindle Edition
ASIN: B006QWS1J8

Childpress **CB** Books

The mission of Childpress Books is to assist parents in forming the moral imagination of children through well-crafted books.

Made in the USA
Lexington, KY
31 October 2016